Linnie's Letters

by Candri Hodges

Cover Illustration: Sue F. Cornelison
Inside Illustration: Sue F. Cornelison

About the Author

Candri Hodges has always enjoyed reading. She especially likes historical stories. Ms. Hodges got the idea for *Linnie's Letters* from reading real-life diaries of pioneer women.

When she is not writing, Ms. Hodges likes to read, go antique shopping, and work in her flower garden.

Ms. Hodges lives in Pennsylvania with her husband, son, and two dogs.

Text © 2000 by Perfection Learning® Corporation.

Printed in the United States of America. For information, contact

Perfection Learning® Corporation

Phone: 1-800-831-4190

Fax: 1-712-644-2392

1000 North Second Avenue, P.O. Box 500

Logan, Iowa 51546-0500.

Paperback ISBN 0-7891-5257-6

Cover Craft® ISBN 0-7807-9666-7

Printed in the U.S.A.

Contents

1

The First Letter

Elinore Frey scrambled through the mercantile doorway and down the porch steps. She plopped down on the bottom wooden step. Then she ripped open the envelope that Mr. Evans had just given her.

Elinore could hardly believe it—a letter from her sister! Tears welled up in her eyes as she began to read.

17 April, 1858

Dearest Linnie,

As I begin this letter, I can't help but wonder if it will ever reach you.

Elinore paused. *Linnie*. The old nickname made her smile. She wiped away a tear that clung to the corner of her eye.

Then Elinore turned back to the letter.

I can only hope that you do receive this letter. With this in mind, I will dip my pen into my ink and continue.

I suppose my writing may come as a surprise to you. I must admit that I myself am a bit surprised. However, I did not realize how very much I would miss you. There is a special bond between sisters. A tender place in a sister's heart that no amount of miles can erase.

Elinore paused again. This time she nodded in agreement. She missed her sister very much too! With a small sniff, she wiped away another stubborn tear. Then she continued reading the unexpected letter.

Are you well, Linnie? Did you reach California unharmed? I pray that you are safe and healthy. I hope you are the same cheerful young girl I remember.

I am doing fine, as is my darling Robert. Oh, Linnie, he is such a wonderful husband. I can hardly believe we have been married almost a year.

Everything is going splendidly for us. We decided to stay on the prairie. We are making our home in the Nebraska Territory.

At first, Robert rented us a room. It was in a small boardinghouse. It wasn't very fancy. Actually, it housed bedbugs and several other unknown critters!

But it was better than sleeping on the hard ground. I think Robert knew that I could not stand another night of "camping."

Elinore smiled again. For her, camping along the Western trail had been fun and full of new adventures. Of course, she and her older sister did not always agree on such things.

Soon after, Robert purchased a lovely piece of land several miles from town. Our kind neighbors gathered on a sunny day. They helped Robert and me cut blocks from the tough prairie grass. We used a special heavy "breaking plow."

We then stacked the earth bricks until we had built a one-room house. We bought a wooden door and covered the windows with oiled paper. I mixed a flour paste and stuck magazine pictures to the walls.

We tore apart our wooden packing crates. We made a small table, a cupboard, a bunk, and two chairs from the crates.

So far, our little sod home has been quite cozy. Patches of spring wildflowers have even sprouted on the grass roof. Of course, if I must tell the whole truth, beetles and mice like to live in the dirt walls.

One morning I found one of the furry little mice swimming inside the water bucket. And last night a disgusting black bug fell right into my corn bread batter. I was not at all pleased.

But Robert simply laughed. He said that the little fellow added an extra bit of meat to our meal.

I will include our address at the end of this letter. I hope you will write and tell me about your new home. Linnie, I must ask you—please do not tell our parents about my letter.

At that, Elinore gulped. How could her sister expect her to keep such a secret? With wide eyes, she continued to read.

I know you may be afraid to do this. We have always been taught to be honest. However, I am not asking you to lie. Only to keep this to yourself if at all possible.

I'm sorry to ask this of you. But I do not wish to communicate with our parents in any way. If they try to share in our letters, I cannot write to you again.

Elinore felt a fresh batch of tears fill her eyes. She didn't want to hide good news from Mama and Papa!

Still . . . it would be far worse if her sister refused to write again! Elinore blinked back her tears so that she could clearly see the letter's next words.

I know it might be hard for you to understand my bitter feelings. But I believe I will never be able to forgive Papa for what he did.

I still cannot believe he left Robert and me on the dusty trail in the middle of the huge prairie! We were all alone. Any number of terrible things could have happened to us.

And no, I cannot forgive Mama either. She did nothing to smooth the fight between Papa and Robert. Nor did Uncle Joseph and Aunt Polly. Though I really did not expect them to help us. After all, it was not their place. I am only their niece.

I am not asking you to understand or to take sides. I am only asking you to write to me. I long to know that you are well and happy. As I said before, I miss you.

I remember the name of the area in California where the wagon train had planned to end its journey. I am sending this letter there. I hope that you will receive it. Please write soon. I will be watching and waiting each day for your letter.

Your loving sister,
Phoebe

LINNIE'S LETTERS

Elinore slowly folded the letter and returned it to its envelope. She held the envelope tightly in both hands and stared across the street. People moved about. They stirred up small clouds of dust as they wandered in and out of the small town's businesses.

But Elinore did not focus on them. She simply stared and remembered that terrible day on the trail.

Elinore's family had all been so excited about the move west. The trip was Robert's idea. "Let's all go together," he said. "As a family."

They had heard lots of wonderful stories about the West. They heard it had rich farmland, growing towns, and even gold.

So everyone agreed. They set out with big plans of starting prosperous, new lives.

But the trip had not been easy. Almost from the very start, Phoebe and Robert had troubles.

Their wagon nearly tipped at a river crossing. One of their oxen tripped and broke a leg. And they ruined two wagon wheels. Simply put, their wagon was too heavy for the journey.

Finally, they left the flat land of the prairie and headed toward the mountains. There, trouble found them again.

The small wagon train began to climb a steep hill. But Robert's team of oxen could not pull its load. Another wheel broke. The wagon slid down the hill, tipping when it reached the bottom.

"You've got to lighten your load," the train leader ordered. "That piano is your problem."

But Robert refused. "I can't leave it behind. It means far too much to me," he replied.

"You don't have any choice," Papa said.

Robert stood perfectly still. He crossed his arms and set his mouth in a stubborn line.

"You'll never get up this hill, nor across the mountains ahead," Papa tried to explain.

But Robert still refused to lighten his load.

"The wagon train will leave you behind," Papa warned. As Elinore watched, her stomach twisted into a hard knot.

"Let the wagon train go," Phoebe spoke up. "Our family will simply travel on our own."

"No," Papa said firmly. "We should not try to cross this trail on our own. That would be foolish."

"But, Papa," Phoebe said. She crossed her arms. "We're family."

Elinore looked from one parent to the other. Her mama's eyes were filled with worry.

"Let the wagon train go on without us," Phoebe argued. "Surely you and Uncle Joseph and Robert can find the way West. We have a guidebook."

Phoebe looked straight at her mother. "You'll stay with us, won't you?"

"No," Papa said again. "The only answer is to lighten your load." He looked at Robert.

Suddenly the train leader loudly cleared his throat. "Well, folks," he said. "You'd best decide. Five minutes—and then we move on out."

Robert took Phoebe by the hand. "Come, dear," he said quietly. "Help me stand our wagon upright."

Mama reached out and stopped Robert. "What . . . what do you plan to do?"

"We'll go back to the prairie town we just left," he replied tightly. "We'll make our home there."

"But Robert," Mama said quietly. "It's only a piano."

"It's *not* only a piano," Robert said shortly. Then he turned and headed toward his wagon.

Elinore watched as Robert led Phoebe away. Three men from the train helped them straighten their belongings.

Within minutes, the wagon train continued its journey west. Elinore walked slowly behind her parents' covered wagon.

Up ahead, Papa drove the team of oxen. His back was straight. His shoulders were stubbornly squared. Mama walked beside the wagon. She faced forward as they moved up the steep hill.

Only Elinore looked back. Tears filled her blue eyes. She watched Robert and her only sister turn around and head in the opposite direction.

A shout interrupted Elinore's memories. She blinked and turned to find her best friend running down the street toward her.

Elinore stood up. She shoved Phoebe's letter into her dress pocket. She quickly wiped away a stray tear and hurried to meet Clara.

2

Secrets

Elinore felt as though she might burst. Her mind raced. She slowly chewed a bite of bread. She longed to tell her mama and papa about Phoebe's letter. How could she possibly keep such wonderful news to herself?

"Aren't you hungry, Elinore?"

Elinore glanced up from her supper plate. "I—I'm sorry, Mama," she murmured. "What did you say?"

Mama gave Elinore a curious look. "I asked if you were hungry. You've barely touched your stew."

Elinore stabbed a chunk of beef. She looked at her mama. Then at her papa. "I suppose I was just thinking," she said softly.

"About what?" Papa asked.

Elinore looked back down at her plate. The uneaten beef was still on her fork. She pushed at her potatoes and onions. "I—I miss Phoebe," she replied.

"We all do," Mama said gently.

"Humph," Papa muttered. "It's her own fault. She should be here with us in California. But that stubborn husband of hers . . ."

"Dear," Mama interrupted quickly.

"Humph," Papa said again. "Robert just couldn't leave that—that piano behind, could he?"

"Well, we can do little about it now," Mama said. She rose from the table and hurried to the stove. "We don't even know where they are."

Elinore swallowed past the lump that suddenly seemed stuck in her throat. She quickly reached for the bread basket. She nearly tipped her tin cup.

But Papa didn't notice. He watched Mama as she spooned steaming stew into a bowl.

"And that's Phoebe's fault too," he grumbled.

"Can't she sit down and write a simple letter? Surely they have mail service on the prairie. For all we know, they may have gone back East."

He frowned at Mama as she set the bowl on the table. Mama returned to her seat. "Families should be together," Papa added. "I'll not forgive her for worrying you so."

"Worrying won't change a thing," Mama said softly. "Perhaps . . ." She sighed and turned to Elinore. "Would you like some preserves, Elinore?" she asked. Mama passed Elinore the crock of strawberry preserves.

"Humph," Papa muttered. He glanced at his wife's sad face. Papa dropped the subject and returned to his meal.

The rest of supper was fairly quiet. Elinore helped Mama clean up the kitchen. Then she excused herself and went to her bedroom.

Elinore sat down at her small desk and pulled a sheet of paper from the drawer. She scooped up her kitten, Tippy. Tippy quickly snuggled into a soft ball in Elinore's lap.

Elinore brushed a lock of her brown hair from her face. Then she began her letter.

22 May, 1858

Dear Phoebe,

I miss you too! I was so excited to receive your

letter. The post office is at the General Mercantile. I sat right down on the porch step there and ripped open the envelope.

I began to cry when I saw it was from you. (Don't worry. They were happy tears.)

Papa says that I cry at the drop of a hat. Mama tells him to hush. She says it is because I am growing into a young lady.

Did you remember that my birthday was this month? On the 13th of May? I am eleven now.

I told Mama and Papa that they should call me by my proper name. I think "Linnie" sounds very babyish, don't you? Mama agreed and calls me "Elinore" all the time now. But sometimes Papa forgets.

I don't mind if you call me "Linnie," though. I am just so, so, SO happy to hear from you!

We are living in a small town. Many of the residents are gold prospectors. But there are quite a few families too. I made a new friend named Clara.

Our town has a school, a church, a land office, a blacksmith, a livery stable, and two hotels. Of course, there's the General Mercantile where the post office is located.

We also have four saloons. Mama promised to punish me if I ever go anywhere near them. She doesn't need to worry. They are disgusting, smelly, loud places.

Papa bought a nice two-story wooden house. He started his barbershop in the front room of the first floor.

Sometimes Mama complains about the way some of the customers talk. "This is our home," she tells Papa. "I don't like Elinore hearing such rough language, especially in her own front room." But I told Mama I had heard it all before on the wagon train.

Uncle Joseph and Aunt Polly live ten miles outside of town. Uncle Joseph says he came west for farmland. I think he just might be caught up in the "gold fever" like lots of other folks out here.

I'm sorry to have to tell you this. Our little cousin Daniel died while we were still on the trail. He was riding on the wagon seat. He slipped off and slid beneath the wheel. He was crushed to death.

Oh, Phoebe, it was so awful! One minute he was bouncing happily and singing a silly song. The next instant he was screaming as he fell to the ground.

I'll never forget it. I still feel terrible whenever I remember. I think that Uncle Joseph will always blame himself for not being able to stop the wagon in time.

Elinore reached for another sheet of paper. She thoughtfully scratched Tippy's head. She laughed when Tippy rolled over on her back.

"I haven't time to play now," Elinore scolded. "Can't you see I'm writing a letter?" The kitten batted at her hand. Then she snuggled back into a cozy ball. Soon the kitten fell asleep.

Elinore smiled and shook her head. She continued to write.

> Your sod house sounds nice. I suppose it is like the ones we passed on the trail. The bugs don't sound nice, though! You should have saved the mouse for a pet.
>
> Mama let me get a kitten. She is one of Clara's cat's babies. She is a pale gray color all over except for the tips of her ears and tail. They are as black as midnight. So I named her "Tippy."

Elinore stopped. She chewed at her bottom lip. She needed to take care with the next part of her letter. Yet, she simply must share her feelings with Phoebe.

Elinore petted Tippy's back. Then she began to write again.

> Please don't get angry about my next question. But I can't help but wonder about Robert's piano. Does it fit inside your one-room house?
>
> I'm not sure if I understand why a piano is so important to Robert. I know it would have been hard to leave it behind. But it was too heavy to keep trying to carry. You broke wheels and tipped the wagon.
>
> And Papa was right. You would never have made it across the mountains with it.
>
> Are you happy with Robert's choice to stay on the

prairie with his piano? Don't you care that he let your family go on without you?

I'm not happy at all! I'm sorry, Phoebe, but I miss you so much!

You are wrong about Papa. He pretends to be angry. But he does not fool me. He is really sad about our family being torn apart.

You are wrong about Mama too. She refused to speak to Papa for almost a week after we left you.

Now I sometimes find her standing alone. She'll be looking out a window or just staring at nothing. I can tell by the sad look on her face that she is thinking of you.

But I will not tell them about your letter. I was lucky enough to be alone when I got it. So they do not know.

It troubles me to hide this from Mama and Papa, though. I feel that is wrong, wrong, WRONG! But I am so happy to hear from you.

I was afraid I would never know where you were. I . . . I even feared that you might be dead. (Oh, I hate to even write that horrible word!)

But, oh, wonderful joy! You are not dead. And I can't wait for you to write to me again. I hope you will tell me all about your cozy little sod house.

Tell Robert I said "hello." Although I'm still angry with him for keeping my sister so far away.

I have filled up all my paper with this letter. So I

must stop writing. I will be sure to buy more before I need it. I still have some money left from selling soap.

Your sister,

Elinore (Linnie)

Tippy suddenly leaped from Elinore's lap and darted beneath the bed. Elinore laid down her pen. Quickly she slid the letter into her desk drawer. A soft knock sounded on the door.

The door opened slowly. Mama poked her head inside the room. "It's close to your bedtime," she said. "But would you like to come into the parlor for a bit? I think your papa would enjoy a game of checkers."

"Yes, Mama," Elinore replied. "I'd like that." Elinore gave her desk drawer a final push. She stood and followed her mama from the room.

3

The Piano

"Let's walk over to the livery stable and visit the new colt," Clara said.

"What for?" Elinore asked. "We've visited that colt two times already. It's cute. But it doesn't really do anything fun or different."

"Well, maybe it's grown some," Clara said.

"In two days?" Elinore looked at her best friend. Clara grinned sheepishly.

"You're not fooling me one bit, Clara. You just want to visit that silly Rufus again. I don't suppose his pa likes us interrupting their work."

Clara leaned close to Elinore and giggled. "Rufus is even cuter than the colt. Don't you think?" she asked.

Elinore frowned. No, she didn't think that. Truthfully, she thought Rufus was a silly boy. She didn't understand why Clara liked him.

And Elinore certainly didn't want to waste her summer hanging about the livery stable talking to him. Even if there was a cute colt to visit. She sighed and looked at Clara.

"Besides," she said, avoiding Clara's question about Rufus. "I need to get on home. Mama wants me to weed the carrots and onions."

Clara wrinkled her nose. "Ew! Who cares about stinky onions anyway?"

Elinore laughed. "I love onions!" she said. "Mama and Papa do too."

And Phoebe especially loves onions, she thought. Elinore smiled. She remembered the onion and butter sandwiches Phoebe enjoyed so much.

Elinore watched as a bird hopped across the dirt street. She thought of Phoebe. She couldn't help but wonder if she had received her letter yet. And more importantly, would Phoebe write to her again? She surely hoped so.

Elinore glanced sideways at Clara. Did she dare tell her about Phoebe's letter? No, Elinore decided. I must keep my word. I can't tell Mama and Papa or Clara.

She looked at Clara. "I'd best be going," she said.

"Oh, all right," Clara said. She brushed a bit of dirt from her dress. "Do you want to come over tomorrow?"

"I don't think I can," Elinore replied. "Mama and I will be busy baking."

"All right. I'll see you later then."

"Mm-hmm—bye," Elinore said as she turned and headed toward home.

The next morning, Elinore helped her mama bake a cake. She carefully scooped flour into the stoneware bowl. Then she stirred as Mama added the rest of the ingredients.

"My land, Elinore," Mama suddenly scolded. "Be careful. You nearly mixed some eggshell into the batter."

Elinore giggled. "That's funny, Mama," she said. "At least it's better th—" She closed her mouth. She'd nearly slipped and told Mama about Phoebe's corn bread batter with its big bug!

"What?" Mama asked.

"Nothing," Elinore mumbled with her head down. She couldn't look Mama in the eye.

"Are you sure?"

"Yes, Mama."

Mama set down her spice tin. She looked at Elinore. "Is something troubling you, dear?"

Elinore refused to meet her mother's eyes. "Not really," she replied. But deep in her heart she knew she wasn't being completely truthful. It really bothered her to keep secrets from Mama and Papa. If only Phoebe would come to her senses!

"Very well," Mama said softly. "But I'm here if you ever wish to talk."

Elinore looked up. "Thank you, Mama."

Mama turned back to her cake batter. She gave it a few final stirs. Then she poured it into the cake pans.

Elinore watched as Mama slid the pans into the oven. Her stomach felt so strange. It felt almost as though she had eaten one of Mama's whole cakes all by herself.

Elinore shook her head and frowned. She had felt perfectly fine until she'd had to cover her mistake with Mama. Could keeping a secret make her feel sick?

Elinore shook her head again. It also began to hurt. Surely that was ridiculous. Still . . . it did seem strange how her stomach and head hurt for no reason.

Mama closed the oven door. She turned to face Elinore.

"There," she said. "We'll let that bake up nice and light." She smiled. "I have a few spare moments. What would you like to do now, Elinore?"

Elinore leaned her elbows on the kitchen table. She rested her head in her hands. "I—I really don't feel well, Mama," she admitted. "Do you mind if I go to bed and rest until dinner?"

Mama hurried over to Elinore. She felt her forehead. "Where are you ill?"

"I'm not sure—all over I guess."

Mama's brow wrinkled with worry. "You go crawl into bed. I'll be in soon."

Elinore did what her mother told her. Soon Mama hurried into Elinore's room.

"Here," Mama said. "I think you're coming down with something. Mrs. Evans told me that lots of folks are sick with a cough and fever. This will help."

Elinore despaired as she watched Mama. Mama opened her jar of goose grease and her bottle of turpentine.

The strong smell filled the air. Tippy jumped down from her comfortable place beside Elinore. She darted from the bedroom.

Mama laughed. "It's not *that* bad," she said, shaking her head.

"But it is, Mama," Elinore complained. "Must we really use that? I'm not coughing. And I don't think I have a fever either."

"It's best to not take any chances," Mama said firmly. "I think you might have a bit of fever. And I heard you coughing last night."

"I didn't *feel* me coughing," Elinore grumbled.

"Of course not, silly," Mama said. She laughed once more. "You were sleeping. And besides, you want to go to the 4th of July celebration next week, don't you?"

"Yes," Elinore said with a frown.

"Then you'd best use this and get all better."

"Yes, Mama," Elinore muttered. But she didn't like it one bit.

Luckily, Elinore did get better. The next week the Frey family joined the town in its 4th of July celebration. There were games and food and all sorts of great fun.

But the very best part of July came near the end of the month when Elinore received her second letter from Phoebe.

26 June, 1858

Dear Linnie,

I have decided to continue to call you "Linnie." Elinore is a fine name. But you will always be "Linnie" to me.

I cannot tell you how happy I was to receive your letter. To know that you are safe has filled my heart with joy.

I am so pleased to hear that you like your home. I'm glad you have made a new friend. (Of course, you always make friends easily with your cheery manner.)

You have a kitten too! How wonderful!

I'm also glad there is a school in your new town. The children here are not so lucky. Promise me that you will study hard and learn everything you possibly can.

I cried when I read about our little cousin Daniel's accident. I often wonder why such terrible things happen.

I hope your birthday was happy. Eleven years old— you are indeed becoming a young lady. But just remember one very important thing. I will always, always, be your BIG sister!

Robert has worked hard to clear our land. He has planted potatoes and corn. I have begun to raise turkeys.

Of course, we still have our team of oxen. And we were able to buy one fine horse. We also have two cows. Robert hopes to buy more next spring.

Robert is so clever! Because of him, I no longer have beetles dropping into my bowls and pots. He tacked muslin all across the ceiling. Now it catches the falling bugs and dirt!

Unfortunately, it wasn't much good last week. We had a horrible storm. The wind howled and the rain beat down.

Our thick sod roof became soaked. There was nowhere for the water to go except down. Through the roof and muslin. On the floor. Down the walls. Everywhere!

You would have laughed to see me, Linnie. I stood at my little stove to cook. I held an umbrella over my skillet. The umbrella protected my frying chicken.

Elinore clutched her letter. She let out a loud laugh. Suddenly, Mr. Evans poked his head through the mercantile doorway. He spotted Elinore sitting on the porch.

"Everything all right, Elinore?" he asked with an amused smile.

"Yes, Mr. Evans," Elinore said sheepishly.

"All right then," he said. "I'd best get back to my customers." He closed the door.

Elinore returned to her letter.

Tomorrow I am going to a quilting bee. Many of us need blankets for winter. We ladies decided to work together.

Whatever did you mean about selling soap? Our soap here is a bit different than what we were used to back East. We have hardly any trees here on the prairie. So we mix cornstalk ashes with the fat instead of wood ashes.

We use corn for practically everything. Mush, flapjacks, bread—what I wouldn't do for a piece of light, white-flour bread!

Yes, Linnie. Robert's piano does fit into our one-room house. We squeezed it into a corner. The top of it acts as a shelf to hold blankets and linens.

I realize it is hard for you to understand completely. But I will try to explain. The piano is not just a musical instrument to Robert.

As you know, Robert's mother died when he was a boy. He was about your age when she died. He remembers his mother sitting on the piano stool. She would play and play for hours. Many nights Robert fell asleep listening to her beautiful music.

The piano is all he has left to remind him of his loving mother.

It is very much like the ruby necklace Mama has. The one that was once her grandmama's. Mama treasures that necklace. She does not care about its value in money. It is priceless to her because it belonged to her grandmama.

It is the same for Robert and his piano. He loves it because it belonged to his mother.

Elinore paused and nodded thoughtfully. She truly wanted to understand. But understanding would not mend her family.

Elinore sighed softly. She continued to read.

I'm sorry that Papa and Robert argued. I'm sorry our family is torn apart. But I am not sorry Robert stood up for something that is so very important to him.

I feel Papa could have tried to find a way to help move the piano. But he rarely thinks of others. He always acts like the biggest toad in the puddle!

I'm sorry Mama is sometimes sad. But she could have convinced Papa. She is the one person he thinks of besides himself. She is the one person he listens to.

I am not sorry Robert chose to stay behind on the prairie while the rest of the wagon train traveled on. He has worked hard to make a home for us.

He is my husband, and I love him dearly. When you are a bit older, you will fall in love and marry. Then you will understand. Please do not be angry with Robert.

I am sorriest about being away from you. I cannot believe a year has passed since we were last together.

I miss our heart-to-heart talks. Our letters will have to be our sisterly chats. Please take care of yourself and write to me often.

> Love,
> Phoebe

Elinore carefully folded her sister's letter. She, too, was sorry about their being apart, and she missed their heart-to-heart talks. She stood and waved quickly to Mr. Evans. Then she hurried home to write to Phoebe.

4

Gold!

30 July, 1858

Dear Phoebe,

The summer is getting so warm. Is it warm on the prairie?

We planted a garden in the spring. I know it is nothing like Robert's fields. But we have fresh onions, green beans, and carrots. And awful cabbage!

Soon we will have corn. But it sounds like you are growing weary of corn.

I wish I could send a loaf of Mama's freshly baked bread to you.

Do you remember me writing that a lot of prospectors live in our town? Well, they are busy panning and digging for gold. They don't have time to bother with making candles or soap or such things.

So Mama and I earn a little household money by making soap. We sell it to Mr. Evans at the General Mercantile. Mama lets me keep a little money to spend however I wish. I bought some new paper and a pen so I could write to you.

I have never heard of making soap from cornstalk ashes. But I suppose if you don't have wood to burn for ashes, the cornstalk ashes would work just as well.

I can't imagine living without trees. I remember how the prairie looked. I remember mile after mile of long, swaying grass.

I hope you don't mind me saying so, but I think California is much prettier than the way I remember the prairie. We have lots of trees here.

If you don't have any trees, what do you burn in your cookstove? I laughed when I read about you holding an umbrella over your head and skillet while you cooked.

I was sitting on the porch of the mercantile. I must

have laughed awfully loud. Mr. Evans stuck his head out the front door to see what was going on.

At the end of June, I got sick. I coughed and had some fever. Mama rubbed goose grease and turpentine all over my back and chest.

It smelled absolutely awful, awful, AWFUL! I choked. It only made me cough more.

I complained about the medicine. Mama said I had to get better before the 4th of July celebration. Otherwise, she wouldn't let me go. So I set my mind to it and got better.

The 4th of July celebration was such fun! I wish you could have been there, Phoebe. There were games and races and turkey shoots.

All the money went into a fund. The town is going to use the fund to build wooden plank sidewalks along the main street. It will be so nice not to have to walk through the sloppy mud and stinky horse you-know-what.

One of the tables sold ring cakes. There were five cakes. Each one had a gold ring baked inside of it. Then slices of cake were sold. If you were lucky, your slice had the ring!

And would you believe it, Phoebe? I won one of the rings!

A boy named Rufus also found a ring in his cake. Do you know what he did with it? You'll never, ever guess. So I'll tell you. He gave it to my best friend, Clara!

Rufus is a silly boy with big brown freckles and blond hair. His hair sticks straight up when he removes his hat.

But Clara giggled and seemed happy when he gave her the ring. She acted almost as silly as he does. But, of course, it is a very pretty ring.

Last week, Tippy chased a mouse. She couldn't catch it. And it was just a teeny, tiny mouse. Papa said not to worry. He was sure Tippy would be a fine mouser before too long.

I almost burst out and said I wished I could send her to you. But I stopped myself in time. Mama gave me a strange look when I clapped my hand over my mouth.

I hate keeping secrets from Papa and Mama. I'm sorry, Phoebe. I can't help but be a little mad at Robert for what has happened to our family.

Elinore paused. Two times she had nearly slipped and told the secret! Perhaps she should show Phoebe's letters to Mama and Papa.

She sighed. No, she dare not. Phoebe would not like that the least bit. Her sister had been quite firm about not writing again.

Elinore frowned. Besides, she had promised. She'd

35

best stay quiet—at least for now. So far they had only written three letters. Perhaps as time passed, she might fix things somehow. Perhaps . . .

Elinore's head began to hurt. Perhaps she should simply not think about it. She would write about other things instead. Elinore sighed again and continued her letter.

Papa is doing quite well with his barbershop. All the rough-looking men are starting to look a little better. Papa laughs. He says that he will clean this town up better than any lawman.

Are there Indians near your sod house? Last week I saw an Indian outside of the livery stable. Rufus said he heard the Indian was looking for some stolen Indian ponies. But I heard Rufus sometimes makes up tales.

Elinore glanced at the last part of her sister's letter. She reread the part that explained about Robert's piano and Phoebe's anger toward their papa. Elinore shook her head. She began to write.

I do understand why Robert's piano is special to him. But I don't agree when you say Papa only thinks of himself.

Just the other week, he closed the barbershop for two whole days. Then he went to help Uncle Joseph

build a fence for his cattle. Family is important to
Papa.

And family is important to me, too, Phoebe.
That's why I'm so happy, happy, HAPPY that we are
writing to each other. I like reading all about you and
your new house. Take care of your turkeys!

Your sister,
Elinore

Elinore quickly folded the letter. She addressed the
envelope. Then she tucked the letter safely inside her
pocket.

Elinore hurried to the parlor. "Mama," she asked.
"Do you mind if I go for a walk until suppertime?"

Mama looked up from her darning. "Of course not,
dear. Just don't be late."

"I won't," Elinore replied. She left the house and
headed to the mercantile. There she mailed her letter.

When she returned, happy shouts and laughter
drifted through the open windows. Elinore could hear
the laughter out on the porch. She smiled. Elinore
recognized her Uncle Joseph's loud voice.

Whatever could be happening? she wondered. She
ran up the steps and through the doorway.

She found her Uncle Joseph and Aunt Polly with
her parents. Fresh lemonade and ginger cookies sat in
the center of the kitchen table.

Elinore's stomach rumbled with hunger. But she ignored the cookies.

She couldn't believe her eyes! There beside the pitcher of lemonade were several fair-sized chunks of gold!

"Is that—?" Elinore began. Her Uncle Joseph jumped up from his chair. He grabbed Elinore. He spun her around and around. Elinore thought she might never see straight again.

"It certainly is," Uncle Joseph said. He laughed as he set Elinore down. "Gold, Elinore, it's gold. What do you think? Your Aunt Polly and I discovered gold on our land. We are going to be rich! Rich, rich, I tell you."

"No!" Elinore exclaimed. Her eyes were wide with wonder.

"Yes," Aunt Polly said, laughing. "Can you imagine?"

Elinore shook her head. Then she leaned closer to the table. "May—may I pick one up?"

Uncle Joseph laughed. "Of course you can." He tossed one of the gold chunks toward his niece.

Elinore grinned. She caught the chunk.

Elinore looked at the piece of gold. She couldn't help but wish that Phoebe were here. Elinore wanted to show her the gold.

"But you have to give it back!" her uncle added, laughing.

Elinore rolled her eyes. "Oh, Uncle Joseph," she said.

Mama pushed back her chair and stood. She smiled at Elinore. "Come on," she said. "Help me get supper on the table. Aunt Polly and Uncle Joseph will tell you all about it!"

5

Little William

The warm summer days slipped past. Elinore
didn't mind. Autumn was her favorite season. It was
late in October now.

One sunny Saturday morning, Elinore waited for
Clara in front of the school. They had decided to spend
the day fishing at Palmers' Creek.

Elinore watched as the small town came to life. Mr. Evans opened the mercantile's doors. Mrs. Tanner bought fresh milk from a farmer. Old Mr. Davis shooed his two cats outside for the morning.

Suddenly Elinore spotted Clara heading her way. "C'mon, Clara," she called. "Hurry up!"

"I'm coming," Clara said. She ran to meet Elinore. "What's your hurry? The fish aren't going anywhere!"

"I know," Elinore agreed. "But I can hardly wait to just sit by the cool creek and do nothing."

"Well, let's get going then." Clara smiled. "I've been looking forward to this too," she admitted.

Elinore picked up the fishing gear. The two girls headed toward the edge of town.

"Did you finish your arithmetic homework?" Elinore asked.

"Yes, it was easy," Clara replied.

Elinore frowned. "Easy for you. I'm still stuck on the third problem. But Mama said I could finish it this evening."

She grinned at Clara. "Did you draw your map for geography yet?"

Clara wrinkled her nose. "No!" She looked at Elinore. "Why do we have to learn all about other countries anyway? It's not likely I'll ever go to any of them."

Elinore shrugged. "I don't know. I suppose it's good to learn all sorts of things."

"Humph," Clara said. She stared at the clouds and sighed. "It's such a beautiful day. It's a shame they can't—look, Elinore. Here comes Rufus!"

Elinore's eyes narrowed. She spotted Rufus walking toward them. She surely didn't want him tagging along to the creek.

"Hi," Rufus said when he reached them.

"Hi," Clara replied.

Elinore frowned at the stupid grin on Clara's face. She'd never understand Clara's feelings for this boy.

"Do you want to play ball?" Rufus asked. "A bunch of us are meeting in the school yard."

"That's awfully nice of you," Elinore began, "but—"

"We'd love to," Clara interrupted. "It's a perfect day for a ball game. Don't you agree, Elinore?"

Elinore frowned at Clara. She certainly did not agree. And she was not going to change her plans. Clara would simply have to tell Rufus "no."

"No," Elinore answered a bit too sharply. "I mean, yes, it's a nice enough day for a ball game. But it's an even better day for fishing."

She turned and gave Rufus what she hoped was a pleasant smile. "I'm sorry, Rufus. It's awfully kind of you to ask. But Clara and I are going fishing."

Rufus shrugged. "All right." He turned to leave.

"Wait," Clara suddenly said. "We can go fishing anytime. We'll play ball today."

Elinore's mouth tightened into a stubborn line. Just who did Clara think she was—making all the decisions? Why was she ignoring Elinore's wishes? Clara knew how much Elinore wanted to go to Palmers' Creek.

Elinore raised her head slightly. She looked at Rufus and then at Clara. "No," she said firmly. "You go ahead and play ball, Clara. I'm going fishing."

And with that, Elinore spun around and marched toward the creek. Her mouth was set in a determined line. Her blue eyes were wet with angry tears.

Elinore sat on the creek's bank. She cast her line into the clear water. "This is great fun," she muttered.

She tried to brush aside her hurt feelings. But she simply couldn't forget how Clara had just tossed away their plans. How could she desert Elinore for Rufus?

And then, to make matters worse, Elinore didn't catch one single fish. She didn't even catch a too-tiny-to-keep one. So she soon packed up her things and headed home.

Elinore passed the mercantile on her way home. Mr. Evans glanced up from his sweeping.

"Oh, Elinore," he called. "There's a letter inside for you."

"Thank you, sir," Elinore mumbled. She forced a smile.

Elinore hurried up the steps and through the doorway. Perhaps it was from Phoebe!

Elinore took the letter from Mrs. Evans. She recognized her sister's writing. Despite her awful morning, Elinore smiled.

Elinore hoped the letter would cheer her up. She settled right down in the corner of the mercantile's porch and began to read.

3 September, 1858

Dearest Linnie,

It's hard to believe that autumn is almost here. Robert will soon harvest our crops. The corn is tall and strong.

Yesterday, Robert pulled a potato plant from the ground. It was loaded with large, firm potatoes.

Robert is so excited. He says we will make enough money to live comfortably through the winter. We will also be able to buy new seed in the spring. Maybe even several more cows.

I am so thankful for that. Because now we have another person living in our little sod house.

Linnie, I have such wonderful, wonderful news for you. You are an aunt! Three weeks ago little William was born.

He is the most beautiful baby I have ever seen. Robert is a proud papa. And I am a very happy mama.

So far, William is a good baby. He is already quite strong. He grips my finger in his tiny fist. He even tries to hold his head up to look around the house.

Elinore looked up. Her eyes were wide. She stared at a small dog barking furiously outside the land office. She could hardly believe it.

An aunt! She was an aunt! To a tiny nephew! It simply didn't seem real. She eagerly returned to the letter.

I'm glad you are feeling all better from your illness. You listen to Mama. Don't complain about her medicines. She knows how to keep you well. I pray that I will be as good a mama to little William.

Elinore chewed at her bottom lip. *William*. That was a nice name. Did they call him "Willy" for short?

It is so clever of you and Mama to make soap to sell to Mr. Evans. I'm glad you have a little money of your own.

Like you, I had never heard of making soap with cornstalk ashes either. But here on the prairie I have had to learn how to do many new things.

We don't have wood for fuel. So we use buffalo chips to build our fires. (Yes, buffalo chips are exactly what you think they are—dried buffalo manure.)

Elinore's nose wrinkled. She continued to read.

The buffalo chips burn very quickly. It is a constant chore to search the prairie for enough to meet our needs. Robert and I gather chips several times a week. Then we store them in gunny sacks in our little sod barn.

Is California windy? The wind always seems to be blowing here in the Nebraska Territory.

It is hot in the summer. In the winter, it is bitter cold.

Doing my laundry is a never-ending battle. I scrub the clothes. Then I hang them on the line.

Unfortunately, the wind coats them with black prairie dust. It is not very pleasant, especially for my new baby's tender skin.

Yes, we do have Indians living near us. My neighbor told me some are dangerous. But mostly they are just curious about the white folks. They think our ways are strange.

Your 4th of July celebration sounded glorious. I do so miss parties. Although our neighbors gather for a bee or picnic once in a while.

Two days ago, three neighbor families came to visit us. They came to see our beautiful William. They brought food and gifts.

We had a lovely time. We talked and ate.

When dusk came, Robert played his mama's piano. Everyone danced and sang.

Thank you for offering to send Tippy to help me with my unwelcome mice. Maybe we will get our own kitten someday.

Family is important to me, too, Linnie. But I'm afraid

I am just not able to forgive Papa and Mama. They left us on the prairie.

However, I must confess. I did especially miss Mama on the day little William was born. Part of me wants to tell Papa and Mama that they are grandparents. Another part of me wants Papa to admit he was wrong.

I must finish my letter. I hear the baby stirring in his cradle. I like to pick him up before he has a chance to cry. (He can really yell when he sets his mind to it!)

I have a busy day planned. I want to make candles. I also plan to gather late berries for jelly.

Robert says "hello." He asks that you please forgive him for making your sister's home so far from yours. He is pleased that you are writing to me.

I believe he wishes Papa and I would somehow make up. But he also respects my feelings. He believes that I must make the choice.

I wish you could see William. I'm sure that you would love him. He would have such fun getting to know his aunt.

Write to me soon. I miss you as much as ever.

> Your loving sister,
> Phoebe

Elinore carefully folded the letter and stood. She hurried home. When she went inside, she stopped.

"What's wrong?" Elinore asked. She looked at her mama's worried face. Then she saw her papa's angry frown.

Mama reached out toward Elinore. "Sit down, dear," she said. Her voice trembled slightly. "We've something to tell you."

"Wha—what is it?"

"Oh, Elinore," Mama cried. "It's so awful. Your papa's been robbed!"

6

Clara's Choice

Several days passed. Elinore finally sat down to answer Phoebe's letter. Thoughts ran through Elinore's mind. There was so much she wanted to tell her sister!

3 October, 1858

Dear Phoebe,

Oh, Phoebe, the scariest thing happened last week!

Papa was in his barbershop. A mean, rough-looking man stumbled through the doorway. Papa said he thought the man looked like he hadn't seen a razor in a long time. What better reason to stop by the barbershop?

But the man wasn't a customer. He looked at all the men waiting for Papa to take care of them. Then he asked Papa if he needed an extra barber.

Well, Papa tried to hide his surprise. Politely, he said no. Papa explained that he could handle his shop by himself.

And then that mean man shocked everyone by pulling out his gun. He pointed it right at Papa's face!

"Well, if ya won't hire me," he shouted, "I'll just have to take yer money the easy way! Give me what's in yer box there!"

Of course, Papa gave him the money. He told Mama the man was a fool. Papa said only a fool would rob a business in the morning. There was no way a business could have made any money that early.

Mama said she didn't care if the horrible man only got a little money. (Papa had only shaved two men before the thief arrived.) She said she'd never heard of a barbershop getting robbed.

Mama said that she hoped you were safe. She was

upset that California isn't as safe as she thought it would be.

I didn't hear the rest of their talk. Papa told me to go outside to the garden. He wanted me to pull a pumpkin. He was longing for one of Mama's wonderful pies.

I finished in the garden and went back in the kitchen. Papa was hugging Mama. When Mama saw me, she pulled away. She took the pumpkin from me.

They didn't say another word about the robbery. But now Papa takes a loaded shotgun to the barbershop every day.

On the same day as the robbery, Clara and I had a fight. It's awful to be fighting with your very best friend.

Clara and I had made plans to meet in front of the school. We were going over to Palmers' Creek to go fishing. I've been so hungry for some tasty fish. Mama said she'd fry whatever I caught for supper.

Well, we were halfway to the creek when we saw Rufus. He asked if we wanted to play ball with some other friends. I started to say no.

After all, Clara and I had been looking forward to fishing. And I could just taste those fish at suppertime.

I stood there shaking my head. Clara saw me too. But she spoke right up. She told him we'd love to play ball.

Clara giggled like a little four-year-old. She

started back toward the school yard. She just ignored me.

Well, I tell you, Phoebe. I was spittin' mad. Madder even than Tippy gets when Uncle Joseph's dog chases her.

Who did Clara think she was? How dare she speak for both of us? How could she choose Rufus over me? I'm her best friend.

So I turned right around and went fishing. Clara skipped off with silly Rufus.

I haven't talked to Clara since. I don't know what she sees in Rufus anyway. Him and his stupid ball games and freckled face.

The day was horrible. I didn't even catch one single fish!

Oh, Phoebe, am I really, truly an aunt? I wish I could see and hold little William. Does he look like you? Or Robert? I am so excited.

It is awfully hard not to tell Mama and Papa. I'm afraid I might burst. They would be so happy to know they are grandparents. It's not fair to keep it from them.

Can you try to draw a picture of the baby? Then I might at least have a tiny idea of how he looks. You used to be able to draw very nice pictures.

I have some wonderful news too! (Though not nearly as wonderful as me having a nephew!) You'll never, ever, ever guess.

Uncle Joseph discovered gold on his ranch! He was digging near his stream. He wanted to make drinking easier for his cattle.

Then he saw a strange shining on the rocks in the water. Sure enough, it was gold!

He has been digging ever since. He really is finding a lot of gold chunks. Some of them are fairly big. Uncle Joseph and Aunt Polly are going to be rich, rich, RICH!

Phoebe, I remember buffalo chips from our covered wagon trip. They were awful!

I always wore one of Papa's old riding gloves before picking them up. Please don't tell me that you TOUCH them with your bare hands.

Now I know I like California better than the prairie. I wish I could send you a wagon full of nice split logs. Then you could burn wood instead of buffalo chips.

Suddenly Elinore felt a soft bump on her elbow. "Tippy!" she scolded. "Get down. I'm trying to write!"

Elinore frowned. Then she gently brushed the kitten from the desktop.

Tippy looked up. She responded with a pitiful "meow." Elinore's frown turned into a grin.

Elinore scooped up Tippy. She held her close. "You rascal. I just can't be angry with you."

Tippy looked at Elinore and purred. She settled herself into Elinore's lap.

Elinore laughed softly. She petted Tippy one last time. Then Elinore turned back to her letter.

This morning Mama and I visited Mrs. Evans and her new baby daughter. (This is the Evans' fifth daughter!) Of course, you know Mama. She could hardly wait to hold the baby.

I held her too. All I could think about was little William. I'm sure he is a much prettier baby than little Sara Evans.

Mama looked at Mrs. Evans. Mama said, "Babies are such a sweet blessin'. But I'll never have another. It's a shame we have to get old." And then she laughed.

Mrs. Evans smiled back at Mama. "Oh, but you'll have grandbabies someday for sure," she said.

Phoebe, it was so strange. Mama's laughter stopped. She looked down at the tiny girl in her arms. She got the funniest look on her face. It was half dreamy and half sad.

"Yes, I suppose I will," she whispered softly. I had to lean forward to hear her. I could tell she was thinking of you—maybe wondering if you would be having babies soon.

Then Mrs. Evans laughed. She said to me, "But you're not in any hurry, are you, Elinore?"

My face and neck got so hot. I know they must have been fire red. I said, "No, Mrs. Evans. I've only just had my eleventh birthday."

At that, Mama glanced at me. The briefest moment passed. Then she laughed.

"No, Elinore's not in any hurry," Mama said. "But I know she'll be a fine mama someday. Having grandbabies to love will be a bit of heaven right here in the wilderness."

I don't think I need to tell you how I felt, Phoebe. I did so wish that I could tell Mama about baby William. It's not right. Mama and Papa should know they have a grandson.

Elinore paused. She truly did want to tell her parents about their new grandson. Sometimes her head hurt from keeping the secret.

Elinore shook her head. She simply must not. Breaking her promise to Phoebe would not be fair.

Elinore pushed aside her troubled thoughts. She finished her letter.

Well! This is surely turning out to be a long, long, LONG letter. We all have exciting lives.

Oh, Phoebe, why do our lives have to be so far apart? I miss you.

It is getting harder and harder for me to understand why Robert doesn't wish to make up with Papa. Why can't he just apologize?

I will only say that I am happy you are pleased with your crops.

And HAPPY BIRTHDAY! I remembered that you will be 19 on the 25th of November.

Kiss and hug William for me. You tell him that his Aunt Elinore sends her love!

Please write soon.

> Love,
> Linnie

Elinore barely finished her letter. She was addressing the envelope when she heard a knock at the back door.

Elinore hurried to open it. She was surprised! Clara was on the porch.

"Oh . . . hello," Elinore said.

"Hi," Clara replied. "Can . . . can you talk for a minute?"

"Yes." Elinore motioned for Clara to step inside.

"I—I hate that we had a fight," Clara blurted. "And then I—I heard about the robbery at your papa's shop." She stopped and studied Elinore's face. "Are . . . are you all right?"

"Yes." Elinore grinned at Clara. "Mama was upset. But Papa thought the whole thing was rather foolish."

Clara smiled too, and nodded. "Will you forgive me? I . . . I'm awfully sorry I tried to be bossy. I shouldn't have played ball with Rufus. I had already promised to go fishing with you."

Elinore's grin stretched into a huge smile. She

reached out and hugged Clara. "Of course I forgive you."

Elinore stepped back. She looked at her friend. "As long as you promise never to do that to me again."

Clara laughed. "I promise."

"Want some cider?" Elinore asked. She went to the cupboard. She took two cups down and poured them each a drink.

"Besides," Clara added. She took a tin cup from Elinore. "You don't have to worry about Rufus anymore."

Elinore's eyes grew wide. "Why?"

"Because—you were right. He is silly," Clara said. "All he ever wants to do is play ball."

"Oh," Elinore said thoughtfully. She drained her cup.

"We had a big fight," Clara added.

"Oh," Elinore said again.

"Do you want to come over for a bit?" Clara asked. "Mother says it's all right."

"OK, but first I must ask Mama." Elinore picked up the cups. She set them in the dry sink. Then she hurried to find her mother.

Elinore grinned as she told Mama about Clara's apology. Then she returned to the kitchen where Clara was waiting for her.

The two girls headed out the door. They were giggling and whispering as usual.

7

Prairie Fire

Autumn turned into winter. The Frey family celebrated Thanksgiving. Then came Christmas. But the holidays just didn't feel quite right to Elinore. Not with part of the family missing.

Elinore watched and waited to hear from Phoebe again. Finally, she received another letter. It was four days after Christmas.

20 November, 1858

Dear Linnie,

I hope you are well. Happy Thanksgiving! I know Mama will prepare a wonderful Thanksgiving feast.

We give thanks in this special month. However, I'm sorry to say that a share of our blessings has been destroyed. A wild prairie fire swept across the land. It burned our acres of fine corn to the ground.

Elinore gasped. A wild fire! She closed her eyes, hoping. Was everyone all right? Phoebe? Robert? Little William? She quickly turned back to the letter. Elinore sighed with relief as she read the next sentences.

Robert says that we will be all right. We were luckier than our neighbors. We still have our potato crop.

It was a miracle. The vegetables beneath the ground were unharmed. I was afraid the heat of the fire would ruin them.

But as I said, it was a miracle. Robert was able to harvest enough to last us through the coming winter.

We are thankful, too, that our house is safe. The cool, damp walls of soddies rarely burn.

And we are especially thankful for our health. No one was hurt in the fire. Robert is tanned and healthy. I am feeling fine. Though sometimes I am quite tired.

Little Willy is growing bigger and stronger every day. Each day I think he gets more beautiful.

I have tried to draw his likeness for you. But no drawing could ever capture his charm.

Elinore picked up two drawings. She had given them a quick glance before. Now she took time to really study them.

Phoebe had not lost her artistic talent. Little Willy was so cute! With one finger, Elinore traced the drawn lines of her small nephew's face.

The other drawing was of her sister's home. How crowded it looked! It seemed as though Phoebe had drawn every detail. She had even drawn Robert's piano squeezed into one corner.

Elinore gave one final glance at Willy's picture. Then she continued to read.

I believe that Willy looks like both Robert and me. He has Robert's black hair and handsome nose. He has my hazel eyes and chin dimple.

Willy's eyes were quite dark blue when he was born. But they are growing lighter every week.

I have also drawn the inside of our little soddy. Hopefully, it will give you some idea of our cozy home.

Imagine! Uncle Joseph finding gold! I'm sure he and Aunt Polly will enjoy being rich.

Have you made up with Clara yet? Next to family, there is nothing quite so important as friends.

Remember, Linnie, that your friendships will change as you grow up. One day, boys will become very important to you. It sounds like they already are to Clara.

Someday you will find that one special boy. You will want to spend all your time with him.

When you marry that special boy, you will put him above everyone else. Just like I did when I stayed on the prairie with Robert instead of going to California with the rest of the family.

I know you don't believe me now. But wait . . .

In the meantime, try to understand Clara. Perhaps Rufus might even become your friend too.

Humph, Elinore thought with a small grin.

Anyway, I smiled when you wrote of Rufus's freckles. I hope that you do not completely dislike them. For Willy has a very large sprinkling of brown dots across his cute nose and round cheeks.

Linnie, when you wrote about fish—my land, what I wouldn't give for a piece of Mama's tasty pan-fried fish.

I'm afraid I must confess to touching buffalo chips with my bare hands. At first I was most careful. I would pick up a chip (folks here call it prairie coal) between two sturdy cornstalks. But that was really quite hard.

Next I tried using one of Robert's worn shirts. But often I would forget to bring the old shirt with me. So I found myself grabbing the chips with the bottom of my apron. This seems to work best for me.

However, (and here is the awful part, dear Linnie!) sometimes I simply forget to use my apron. Without thinking, I shove my hand into the fuel bucket. I grab a chip and toss it through the oven doorway.

I do try to always wash my hands when I have finished this chore. I hope I never forget the fact that my fuel is really buffalo waste.

I know it is a strange way to keep a fire. But whatever would I do without the buffalo chips? I need them to warm my home, heat water, and cook.

Touching buffalo chips is only one of the changes in me. I am not quite the same big sister that you knew before our separation.

I've learned to adjust to this harsh prairie. It has changed my ways of daily living.

It has also changed my appearance. The steady wind and hot sun have destroyed my lovely dresses. They have faded until I can barely see their soft calico prints.

My skin, too, has taken a beating. My face is so dry and lined. It looks like Papa's rough leather razor strap.

My hair has no shine or life to it at all. Why, it almost feels like straw!

Robert says, "Balderdash, you are exaggerating,

Phoebe dear. You are as pretty as the day I married you."
But I fear he is simply being kind.

Elinore lowered the letter. Was it true? Surely her
sister could not have changed so much. And yet, the
things Phoebe had described—the buffalo chips, the
harsh weather—were certainly different. Even
unpleasant.

Elinore shook her head. Perhaps Robert was right.
Phoebe was simply exaggerating.

Your report of the robbery in Papa's barbershop
worried me! I'm so very relieved no one was hurt. I agree
with Mama. I have never heard of anyone robbing a
barbershop either. How foolish!

I'm not sure what to say about Mama's visit with the
Evans' new baby girl. I'm sorry she seemed sad to you. I
know she would fall madly in love with little Willy.

But it is her and Papa's stubbornness that has kept us
apart. I must confess. I am deeply hurt that neither one
of them has tried to contact Robert and me.

For all they know, we could both be starving and
homeless. We could be sick or even dead!

Papa should really stop and think about how he left
us behind. He would probably see his mistake. But as I
said before, Papa thinks only of himself.

Once again, I beg you not to blame Robert for the

distance between us. Several times he has told me how very bad he feels about fighting with Papa. He is sorry that his piano has caused such a problem.

Robert has even suggested (sometimes rather strongly) that I should write to Papa and Mama. He thinks I should try to make things right.

But I have firmly refused. I believe he was right to voice his opinion.

Papa needs to realize that I am an adult now. Robert and I may be young. However, we should still have a say in important matters.

But we have written of this before. I do not wish to keep thinking about it. I feel it makes our letters a bit sad.

It only reminds me how much I miss you. It makes me wonder if I will ever see you again.

Robert has just come in from feeding the livestock. He is now reading over my shoulder. He says "hello" and sends his love.

I, too, send my love. I can hardly wait to receive your next letter. I want to hear all about your adventures in wild California.

Love,

Phoebe

P.S. Thank you for the birthday greeting!

8
The Long Winter

Frowning, Elinore laid Phoebe's letter aside. She went to her desk. She pulled out some paper and her pen.

Elinore brushed a lock of hair away from her eyes. She began to write. Her face was set in determination.

29 December, 1858

Dear Phoebe,

How awful about your fire! I'm so glad that you and Robert and Willy are safe. And I'm happy that Robert was able to save enough of his potato crop. Now he'll be able to take care of you through the winter.

Thank you for the wonderful, wonderful drawings. I used to have a hard time imagining your little soddy.

I've studied your drawing. Now I can picture everything—the packing crate furniture, your cookstove, your muslin-covered ceiling, and even the thick dirt walls.

And the drawing of Willy! Why, he is simply cute, cute, CUTE!

I'm happy to say that Clara is my best friend again. She had a big fight with Rufus. She even gave his gold ring back to him.

Well, actually she threw it in the wood bucket beside the stove at school. And that mean old boy acted like he didn't even care.

Rufus just felt around the bottom of the bucket. Eventually, he found the ring. He wiped it off on his flannel shirt.

Then Rufus turned right around and gave the ring to Janie Woods!

I understand what you wrote about choosing

Robert over the family. However, I can't help but wonder why you should have to choose at all? Why can't everyone be together so no one has to choose sides?

Anyway, I can't believe that you look as terrible as you say. Perhaps you can rub some cream or something on to your skin to make it soft.

You have always been so very, very pretty. I'm sure that Robert is right. You must be exaggerating.

And remember what Mama always says. Wear your bonnet!

I'm not a very good artist. But I tried to draw a picture of Tippy for you. I hope you like it.

I don't know why Mama and Papa haven't tried to reach you. But if you really think about it—where would they look? I would never have known where to write you if you hadn't written first.

I hope that you had a merry Christmas. We had a great big tree. We hung cookie ornaments on it. We also burned candles in our tin holders.

Papa read the Christmas story about Baby Jesus. I knitted Papa a bright red scarf. I bought Mama a new set of hair combs.

My present was my very own checkerboard and checkers. I have already beaten Papa in three games. Mama is still better than both of us. She always, always wins.

My stocking was filled with dried fruit and nuts.

And Uncle Joseph and Aunt Polly gave me my very own gold nugget.

Tippy even got a gift. She got a brand new stuffed ball. It was made from one of Papa's old wool stockings.

The day before Christmas, Mama and I made taffy. Oh, Phoebe! All I could think about was you.

Remember how we would sit at the table and pull the taffy? Mama would decide when it was just right. I can't believe we have spent two Christmases apart!

I miss you so much. At the same time, I am so upset with you. Because now I know the truth!

I'm glad you told me how sorry Robert is about arguing with Papa. Now I know that he wishes we could all forgive each other.

You are just as bad as Papa. No, you are WORSE than Papa. You say that Papa should admit he was wrong. Don't you think that perhaps you were wrong too?

Robert admits he was wrong. Still, you will not. You are just too stubborn, stubborn, STUBBORN!

You say Papa needs to realize that you are an adult now. Well, I'm sorry, Phoebe. I know I am only eleven— much younger than you. But you don't seem to be acting like an adult at all. I think you are acting like a big baby!

Elinore paused. She bit at her lower lip. Perhaps she was being too mean. Maybe she should keep her thoughts to herself.

She frowned. No, she could not let this problem continue. She could not keep hiding the truth from Papa and Mama. With determination, she began to write again.

Poor, precious little Willy. How I long to see my sweet nephew. But I cannot because you are so stubborn!

Why can't everyone forget what has happened? Why can't everyone apologize so we can be a happy family once more? Why?

I am sorry, Phoebe. I cannot go on lying to Mama and Papa.

I will not say anything until I hear from you again. But you must tell Mama and Papa where you are. Otherwise, I will tell them.

Perhaps I should not send this letter with its mean words. But we have always been able to share our feelings. That is simply what I am doing.

I truly do hope that you are all doing well. Please tell Robert I miss him. Give Willy a big, big, BIG hug.

Your sister,
Elinore

The winter months slipped slowly by. Elinore watched and waited. No reply came from Phoebe.

Elinore worried as more time passed. She often stopped by the mercantile, hoping for a letter.

Spring came. The rainy weather only made Elinore feel worse. One dreary afternoon, she headed home from school.

Dark clouds from an earlier storm still hung overhead. Elinore made her way down the street. A strong wind blew a cold mist into her face.

Elinore looked up at the clouds. She pulled her coat collar up over her ears. She hurried home.

Elinore finally reached her yard. She ran up the steps, across the porch, and through the doorway.

"Mama," she called. "I'm home!"

"I'm in here, dear," came the reply. "In the parlor."

Elinore hurried to the parlor. She found her mama sitting on the settee. One of her legs was propped on a stool. The stool was piled high with soft pillows. More pillows were tucked behind her back and shoulders.

"Mama!" Elinore cried. She rushed to her mother's side. "What happened?"

"Oh—silly me," Mama said with a small smile. "Earlier, during the storm, I went outside. I fell on the slippery sidewalk. One of Papa's customers ran and fetched the doctor."

Mama made a funny face. "My leg's broken in two places."

"Oh, Mama, no." Elinore knelt beside her mother and took her hand. "Does it hurt terribly?"

Mama smiled softly. "Not too bad. Doc Drake gave me some pain medicine. It surely helps. But I feel a bit sleepy."

She squeezed Elinore's hand. "I'll need your help with household chores."

"Don't worry. I'll help," Elinore promised.

"All right—thanks, dear." Mama squeezed Elinore's hand again. Then she leaned her head back and closed her eyes.

Elinore did help her mama. She cooked and cleaned. She even did laundry. But between chores, she thought of her last letter to Phoebe.

Perhaps she had been wrong to send it. Perhaps it had been too mean. She couldn't bear to wait any longer. So one evening she wrote another letter.

30 March, 1859

Dear Phoebe,

Please forgive me! I have been waiting and waiting for your letter. But none has come.

Now I realize that you must be quite angry. I had no right to criticize you. I should not have written those terrible things.

Of course you are allowed to have your own feelings. I apologize for writing such a mean-spirited letter.

Spring is here. Our winter was not rough. Still, I am glad that it is over.

Papa continues to do well in his barbershop. Uncle Joseph and Aunt Polly continue to find more gold. Aunt Polly also tells us that we shall have a new cousin sometime in August.

Mama has had a most unfortunate accident. One rainy, stormy day she slipped on the wet wood of the new plank sidewalk. The sidewalk runs in front of our house.

She fell and broke two bones in her right leg. Doc Drake fixed her up. Now she is healing nicely.

I have taken over the chores of cooking and cleaning. My work cannot compare to Mama's. But Papa and Mama both say that I am doing well. They seem to understand that I am trying to do my very best.

Please, please forgive me, Phoebe. Write soon. Tell me that we are friendly sisters once more.

> Your loving sister,
> Linnie

9

A Letter from Robert

Again, Elinore waited. Then one day, she finally received a letter. She sat down on the mercantile porch. She eagerly ripped open the envelope.

The letter's postal markings were familiar. The handwriting was not. Elinore quickly glanced at the signature.

Fear gripped her. Why was Robert writing and not Phoebe? Had something terrible happened to Phoebe?

5 May, 1859

Dear Linnie,

I received your letter. I sat down to write to you right away. You are mistaken. Phoebe is not angry or upset with you. I should have written to you sooner. But I simply did not think to do so.

You see, Linnie, I have been nursing your sister back to health. She has been quite ill. I was so scared that I might lose her.

Phoebe was unable to answer your December letter. She was struck with a chill. Then she got a terrible headache and fever.

Soon she became delirious. I didn't know what to do. I rode for our closest neighbor.

The neighbor woman returned with me. She looked at Phoebe briefly. She told us that Phoebe had the ague.

The ague is a kind of fever. It meant that Phoebe would have fits of chills, fever, and sweating. I was very worried.

Our kind neighbor gave me detailed instructions

on how to care for your sister. I was most grateful for her help. We have no doctor for miles around.

It was a most uncertain time for us. But I am happy to say that Phoebe is getting better. She is still quite weak. But she is growing stronger each day.

I am thankful that neither Willy nor I have caught this illness. Willy continues to grow. He has developed a little lopsided grin. It reminds me very much of you.

Other than Phoebe's illness, our winter has been satisfactory. For that I am also thankful.

As soon as we received your second letter, Phoebe made me sit down and write. Phoebe is not angry. She has always valued her relationship with you—especially the openness the two of you share.

I must confess, Linnie. During the past two months, I have been thinking about things quite seriously. Now I have made a decision about what I must do.

I have sent a letter for your parents. Please deliver it to them for me. It explains how Phoebe's illness and your letters have helped me.

I now realize how very important family is. It is far more important than anything else—even my piano.

Please feel free to tell your mama and papa all about Phoebe's letters.

Please do not worry about your sister. I promise that she will be as good as new before too long.

Please write soon. Phoebe is most anxious to hear from you. (I, too, have come to look forward to your cheery letters.)

Your faithful brother-in-law,
Robert

P.S. Phoebe has just reminded me to wish you a happy birthday!

Elinore sniffed and wiped happy tears from her cheeks. She jumped up and ran home to tell her parents the news.

10

Together Again

Elinore sat beneath the large oak tree in the backyard. The summer breeze rustled the thick leaves. It tugged at Elinore's brown hair.

Elinore chewed on her bottom lip. She thought back over the events of the past weeks. She began her letter.

25 August, 1859

Dear Phoebe (and Robert and Willy too!),

I miss all of you so very, very much. I thought that seeing you would make the distance between us easier. But I find I miss you all the more now that you have returned to your little soddy on the prairie.

Elinore thought back to earlier that week. She, along with Mama and Papa, had stood on the stage depot porch. They had waved until the stagecoach disappeared from sight.

The stagecoach carried Phoebe, Robert, and Willy back to the Nebraska Territory. Their visit to California had been so very wonderful. And far too short.

I'm sure the residents of our small town will speak of your visit for a long while. They all loved each of you—especially Willy with his constant giggle and lopsided grin. (I hate to admit it. But I must agree that his grin does look like mine in a small way.)

I want you to know that your visit has made all the difference to Mama and Papa. Sometimes I catch Mama smiling for no reason. And often I hear Papa whistling as he trims a customer's hair.

Elinore grinned. She could not even come close to describing the change in their lives. They were all so happy now.

They had arrived three weeks ago. Just as Robert's letter to Elinore's parents had promised. Elinore held her breath as Phoebe and Robert stepped down from the stagecoach. Would there be an argument and more hurt feelings? Elinore had wondered.

But Elinore need not have worried. Phoebe spotted Papa and Mama first. She handed little Willy to her husband. Then she flew into Papa's open arms.

Tears streamed down Phoebe's cheeks. She hugged Papa and then Mama. Then she had turned slightly.

Phoebe was looking for Elinore. Elinore threw her arms around her older sister. She hugged with all her might.

"Thank you, Linnie," Phoebe whispered. "Thank you."

There was a short round of apologies. Finally, everyone laughed.

They turned to find Robert and Willy watching them. With huge smiles, they had reached out and drawn Robert and Willy into the family circle.

A pesky fly pulled Elinore back to the present. She impatiently swatted the fly away. She continued her letter.

I'm not supposed to say anything. Papa is afraid to build up everyone's hopes. But I am just so, so, SO excited. I fear I might burst!

He has hinted that he hopes all goes well with our finances throughout autumn and winter. Perhaps then we may be planning our very own visit to you and your soddy next summer.

Mama has framed your picture of Willy. She hung it in the parlor.

Mama is so proud of her grandson. She talks about him to anyone who will listen.

And Papa! He is almost worse than Mama! Sometimes, I help out by sweeping the barbershop floor. I hear him going on and on about little Willy.

I can't help feeling sorry for the poor customer. He is sitting in the chair and cannot get away from Papa's endless bragging.

"You should see the hair on that young 'un!" Papa exclaims. I simply smile helplessly at the poor soul in the barber seat.

How I wish that all of you could have stayed here to live. But I do understand the prairie is now your home. I realize you have come to love it.

I know you feel you must return and continue the life you have worked so hard to build. I pray that Papa's plan becomes real. I would love to see your wonderful farm.

How is your new kitten doing? She is so very cute, cute, CUTE! I hated to see her go.

But I know that she will be a big help in your sod house and barn. No more furry mice swimming in your water bucket! She will be good company too.

Would you believe? Crazy Tippy does not even act as though she misses her baby at all!

I miss all of you. (I know I said that before.) I wish I could hold my little nephew again. He will grow so much before the next time I see him.

And you, Phoebe. It was so wonderful to have our silly talks like we used to do.

Elinore put down her pen. She stretched her fingers. Then she plucked a clover flower from the thick grass.

Of course she missed her sister and baby nephew. But she missed her brother-in-law too.

Elinore remembered the evening when she and Robert had sat at the small parlor table.

"It's your turn, Linnie," Robert said. He grinned as he jumped and captured two of Elinore's checkers.

Elinore slid another one of her checkers into the home row. "King me," she said, grinning back.

Robert shot Elinore a teasing frown. He kinged her checker. Then he leaned forward to study the checkerboard.

"Robert," Elinore began slowly.

Robert glanced up. "Yes?"

"Did . . . did you mind terribly—selling your piano?" Elinore asked quietly.

Robert smiled. His eyes held a touch of sadness. "Truthfully, watching the new owner carry it away was a bit hard. But did I mind selling it?"

He looked toward the settee where Phoebe and Papa chatted. And then his eyes dropped to Willy. Willy was curled up and fast asleep in his grandpapa's lap. "No," he said slowly. "The piano was very special to me. But sometimes we must choose what holds the most value."

Elinore nodded. She gave Robert an understanding smile.

"And I have you to thank, Linnie," Robert said softly. "Your letters made Phoebe—and especially me—realize how foolish we'd been." He smiled again. "Thank you, Linnie."

Now Elinore sat beneath the oak tree. She tucked the memory away in her mind.

Elinore tossed the clover flower into the breeze.

She picked up her pen and returned to her writing.

I miss Robert as well. When I grow up, I hope to marry a man as fine as Robert. What he did was the most generous and kind thing I have ever known. I will always be grateful that he was willing to part with his piano so that our family could be together again.

Thank him again for selling his beloved piano so that you could pay for your trip to California.

I'm glad he shared his change of heart with us. His firm belief that families are far more valuable than any material possession is so true. It is truly a blessing to have our family back together and loving once more.

Please write to me soon. Tell me all your prairie news. Give Willy a big, big, BIG hug and kiss from his Aunt Linnie.

> My love to you all,
> Linnie

Elinore set the letter aside. She carefully addressed the envelope. Quickly she finished the task. She stood and brushed off her skirt.

Elinore hurried to the kitchen window. She called, "Mama, may I go to the mercantile to mail my letter to Phoebe?"

Her mother's pleasant "Of course, dear. Don't be too long" drifted out onto the back porch. Elinore left her ink and pen on the small outside table.

Elinore walked around the house. She waved quickly to Papa through the barbershop window. Elinore smiled to herself and headed down the street.